JUST A D.
AT THE POND

BY MERCER MAYER

To the elves . . .
Diane, Bonnie, and Rita!

 HarperFestival®

A Division of HarperCollinsPublishers

HarperCollins®, ♠®, and HarperFestival® are trademarks of HarperCollins Publishers.
Copyright © 2008 Mercer Mayer. All rights reserved. LITTLE CRITTER, MERCER MAYER'S LITTLE CRITTER and
MERCER MAYER'S LITTLE CRITTER and logo are registered trademarks of Orchard House Licensing Company. All rights reserved. Printed in the United States of
America. For information address HarperCollins Children's Books, a division of HarperCollins Publishers, 1350 Avenue of the Americas, New York, NY 10019.

Library of Congress catalog card number: 2008922488

A Big Tuna Trading Company, LLC/J. R. Sansevere Book

www.harpercollinschildrens.com   www.littlecritter.com

❖

First Edition

I went to Grandma and Grandpa's to spend a day at the pond. Little Sister came, too. Mom and Dad were going shopping. They would pick us up later.

Little Sister went with
Grandma to make a
picnic lunch.

I went to the shed to pick out some fishing poles with Grandpa.

Grandpa put a wagon on the big
tractor for us to ride to the pond. I
drove, but not by myself.

We picked a great picnic spot. Little Sister wanted to go swimming, but I wanted to go fishing first.

I put a worm on the hook.
It was slimy.

I waited and waited for
a fish to bite my worm.

Suddenly . . .

. . . something was tugging on my
fishing line. It was pulling me into
the water.

"Help, Grandpa," I yelled.

Then the line broke.
I thought it was a shark,
but it was just a turtle.

Little Sister was swimming with Grandma.
"Teach me to swim, Grandpa," I said.

I ran to the waters edge, but
then I changed my mind.

I wanted to catch frogs instead.

I found a bunch of frogs.

I snuck up on them very quietly.

But the frogs were too fast.

I was all muddy.

Grandma had to pour a million
buckets of water over me.
   "Oh, look!" she said. "Little Sister
is swimming so well with Grandpa."

I could swim if I wanted to, but I decided to explore instead. I found a good hiking stick.

I found a hole in the ground. I stuck my hiking stick into it. Something made a buzzing sound.

It was ground bees. I
ran as fast as I could.

Grandpa came and got me.
We jumped into the pond and
the bees went away.

I was floating. I
kicked my feet . . .

. . . and paddled my arms
as fast as I could. I was
swimming with Grandpa.

I swam with Grandma
and Little Sister, too.

"Wow, Grandpa," I said.
"I guess I can swim after all."